C0-BKX-615

Copyright © 1992 by David Juniper. All rights reserved under the Pan-American and
International Copyright conventions.

This book may not be reproduced in whole or in part in any form or by any means,
electronic or mechanical, including photocopying, recording, or by any information
storage and retrieval system now known or hereafter invented, without written
permission from the publisher.

Canadian representatives: General Publishing Co., Ltd., 30 Lesmill Road, Don Mills,
Ontario M3B 2T6.

International representatives: Worldwide Media Services, Inc.,
115 East Twenty-third Street, New York, NY10010.

9 8 7 6 5 4 3 2 1

Digit on the right indicates the number of this printing.

ISBN 1-56138-135-7

Cover design by David Juniper
Interior design by David Juniper
Title page and back cover photography by Gareth Winters
Technical and historical information by N. J. Downend, The Booking Hall, London
David Juniper is represented by Folio Artists' Agents, London and New York
Printed in Hong Kong

This book may be ordered by mail from the publishers. Please add $2.50 postage and
handling. *But try your bookstore first!*

Running Press Book Publishers
125 South Twenty-second Street
Philadelphia, Pennsylvania 19103

ALL ABOARD

Four
Railway Legends
For You
To Assemble

David Juniper

Running Press
Philadelphia, Pennsylvania

INTRODUCTION

I have created this book as a tribute to the era of steam power. I offer these models of four of the world's most famous railway trains for your enjoyment.

These giants of the iron road, whistles blowing and smoke speeding from their stacks, hauled comfortable coaches in which travelers could dine, sleep, and enjoy the ever-changing scenery. This form of transportation has been preserved by railway enthusiasts, who have restored engines, coaches, and rail lines to their former glory.

The models in this book, although not exactly to scale, capture the detail and styling of the trains on which they are based. The models are easily assembled; they are die-cut for easy removal and require no glue. Assembly instructions are provided in the pages for each model.

I would like to thank Nicholas Dawe of Folio for his help and support during this project, and Nigel Downend of the Booking Hall, London, for his invaluable aid with the technical and historical information included in the text. My special thanks to Alastair Campbell for his help in the preparation of this book.

David Juniper

C

A

B

MALLARD   MALLARD

Nº 4468

E

Lift gate-fold

Lift gate-fold

A

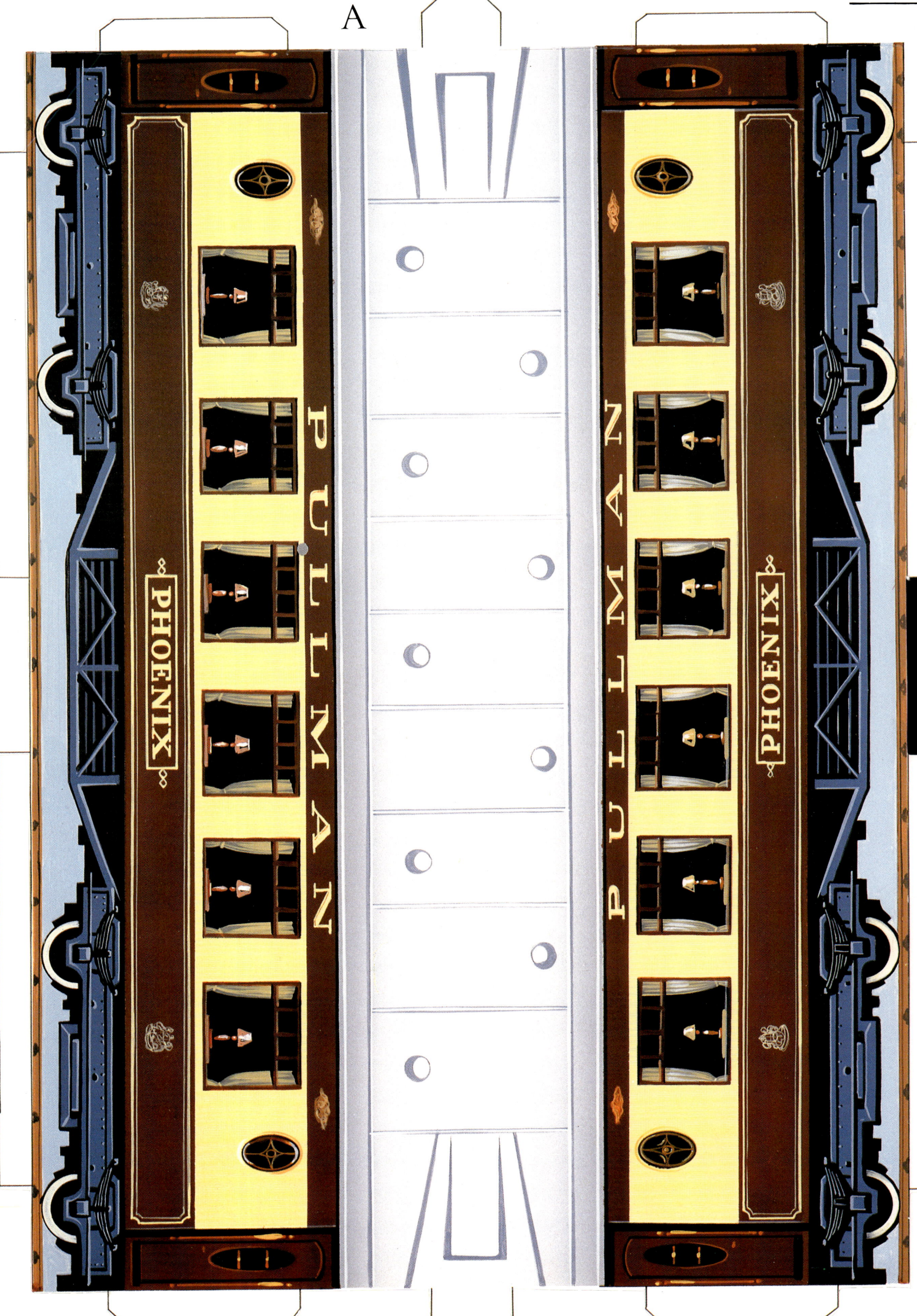

Mallard

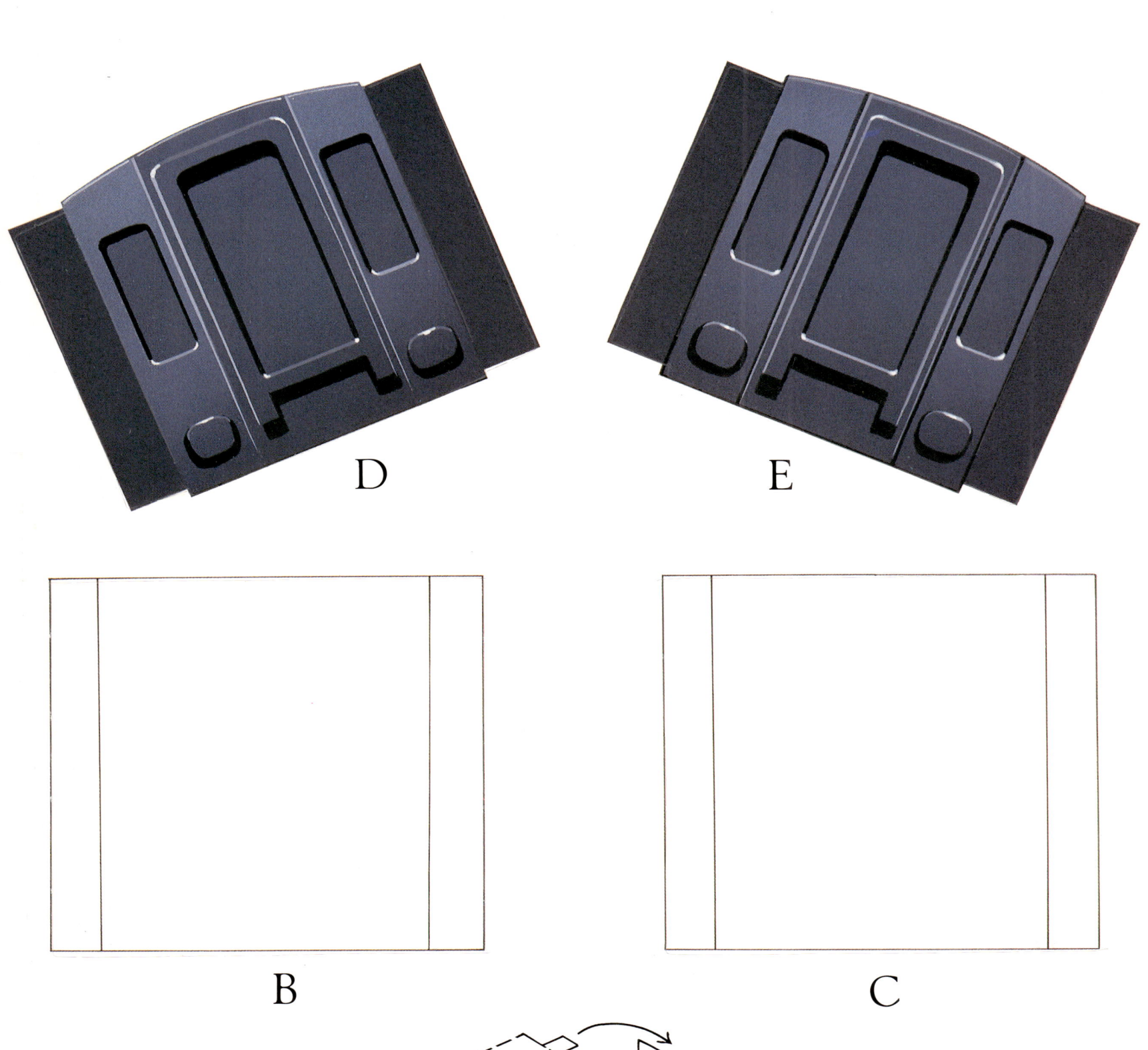

D

E

B

C

(A)

(D)

(B)

(C)

(E)

1. Remove all the parts.
2. Fold main section
(A) as shown. 3. Slot
struts (B) and (C) into section
(A). 4. Slot end sections (D) and
(E) into section (A).

1. Remove all the parts. 2. Fold main engine section (A) as shown. 3. Slot engine section (B) into section (A).
4. Slot struts (C) and (D) into sections (A) and (B) as shown. 5. Fold boiler section (E) and slot into sections (A) and (B). 6. Slot front lamp (F) through section (E) and into section (A). 7. Slot cab roof (G) into sections (A), (B), and (E).

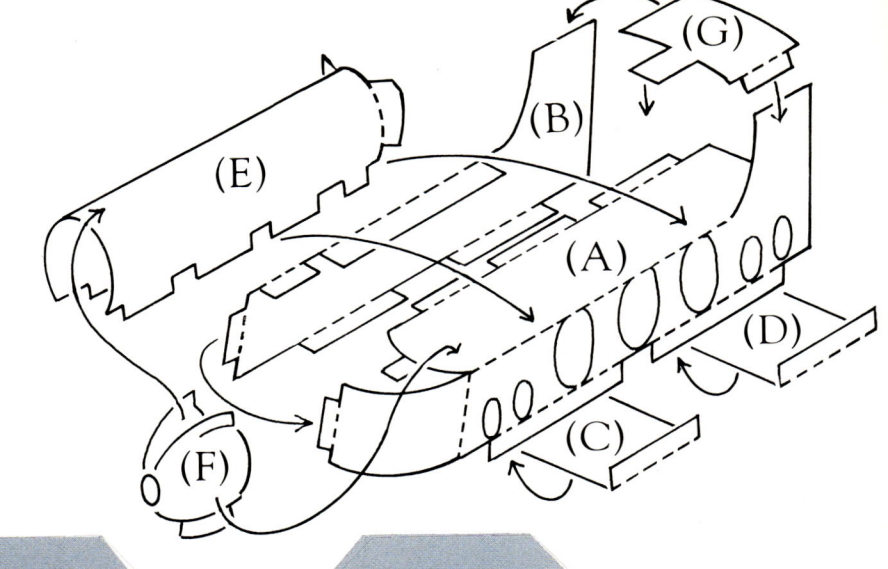

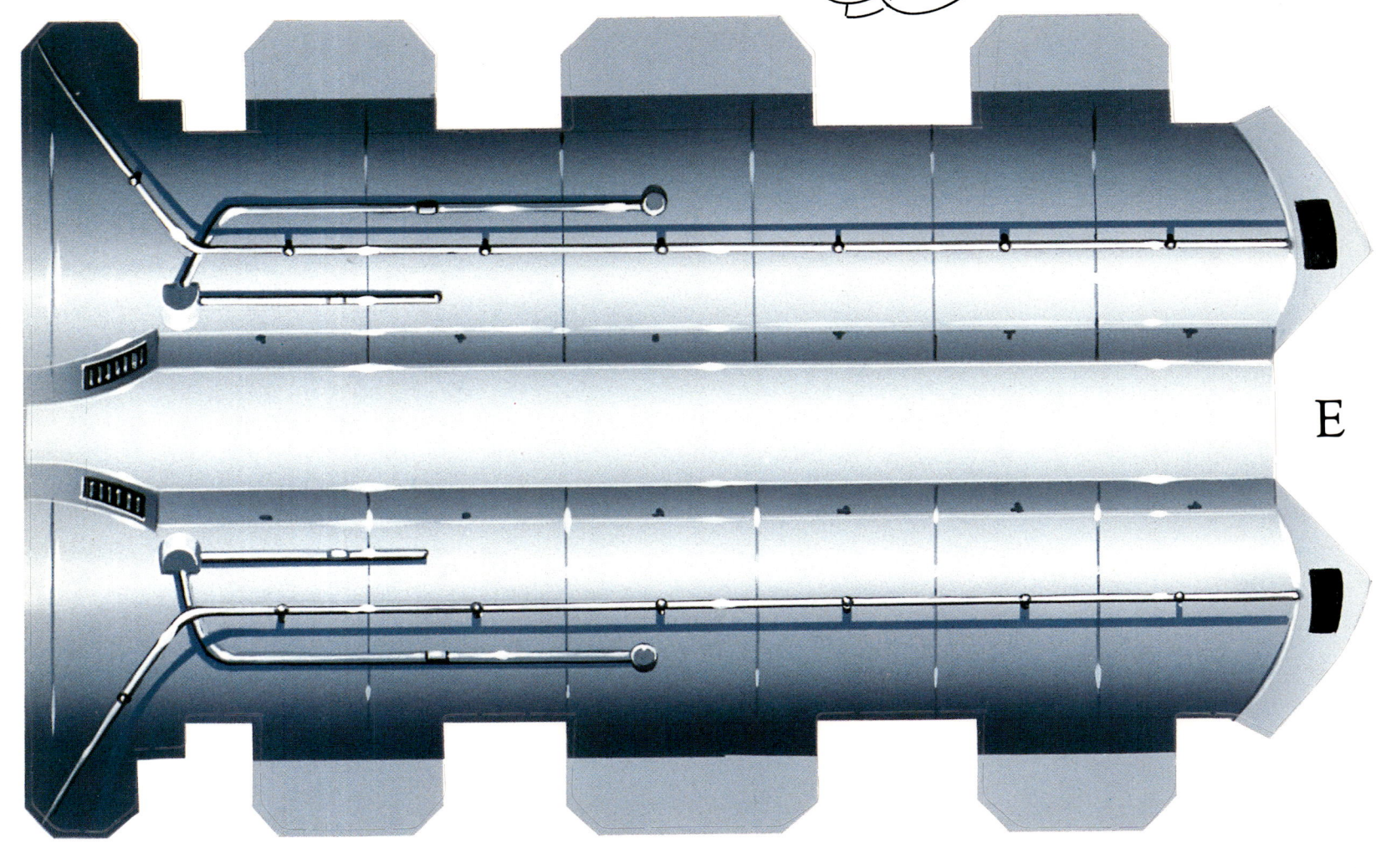

E

J CLASS HUDSON
4 - 6 - 4
STREAMLINED
LOCOMOTIVE

20th

Lift gate-fold

Lift gate-fold

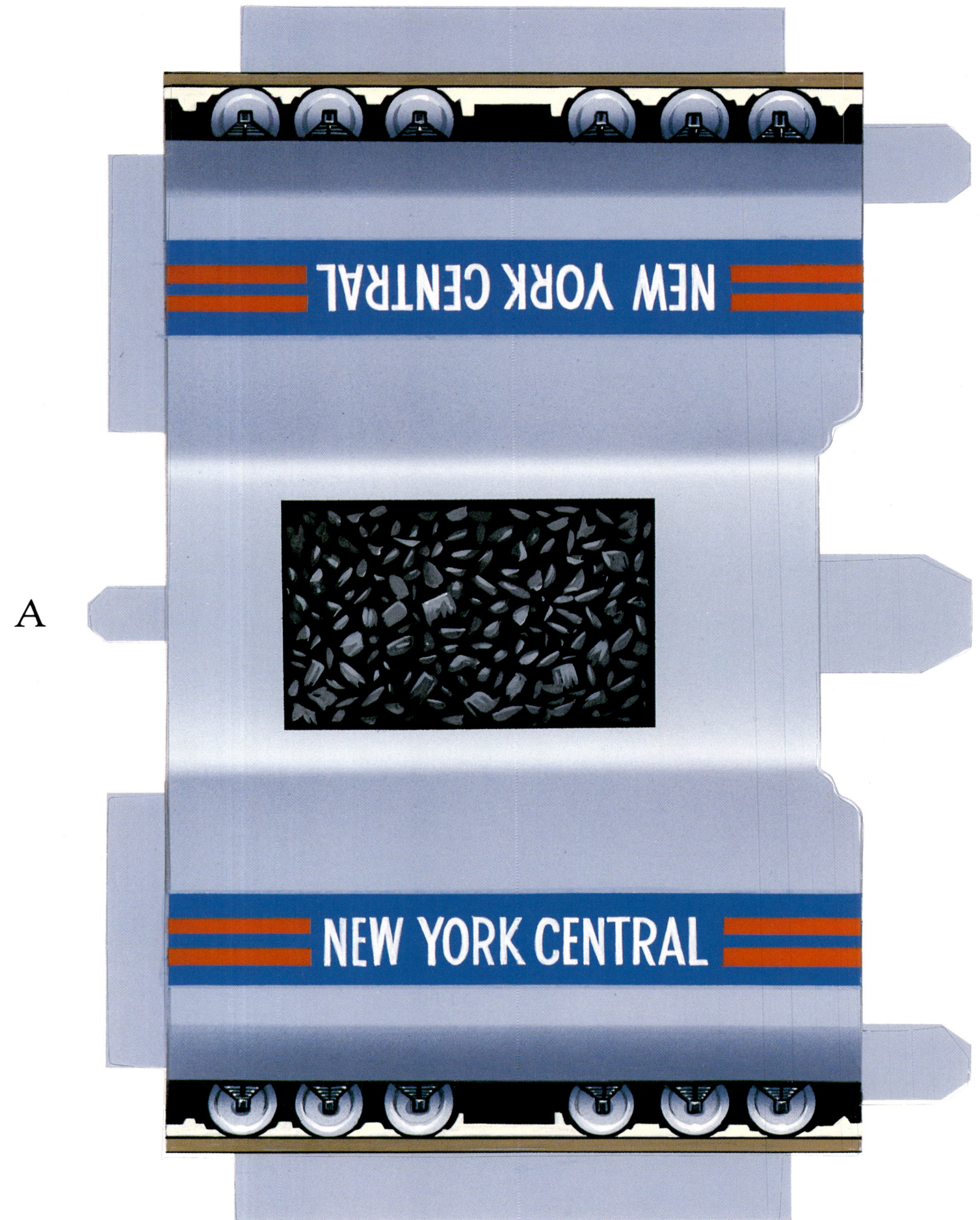

A

NEW YORK CENTRAL

TENDER

20th Century Limited

C

B

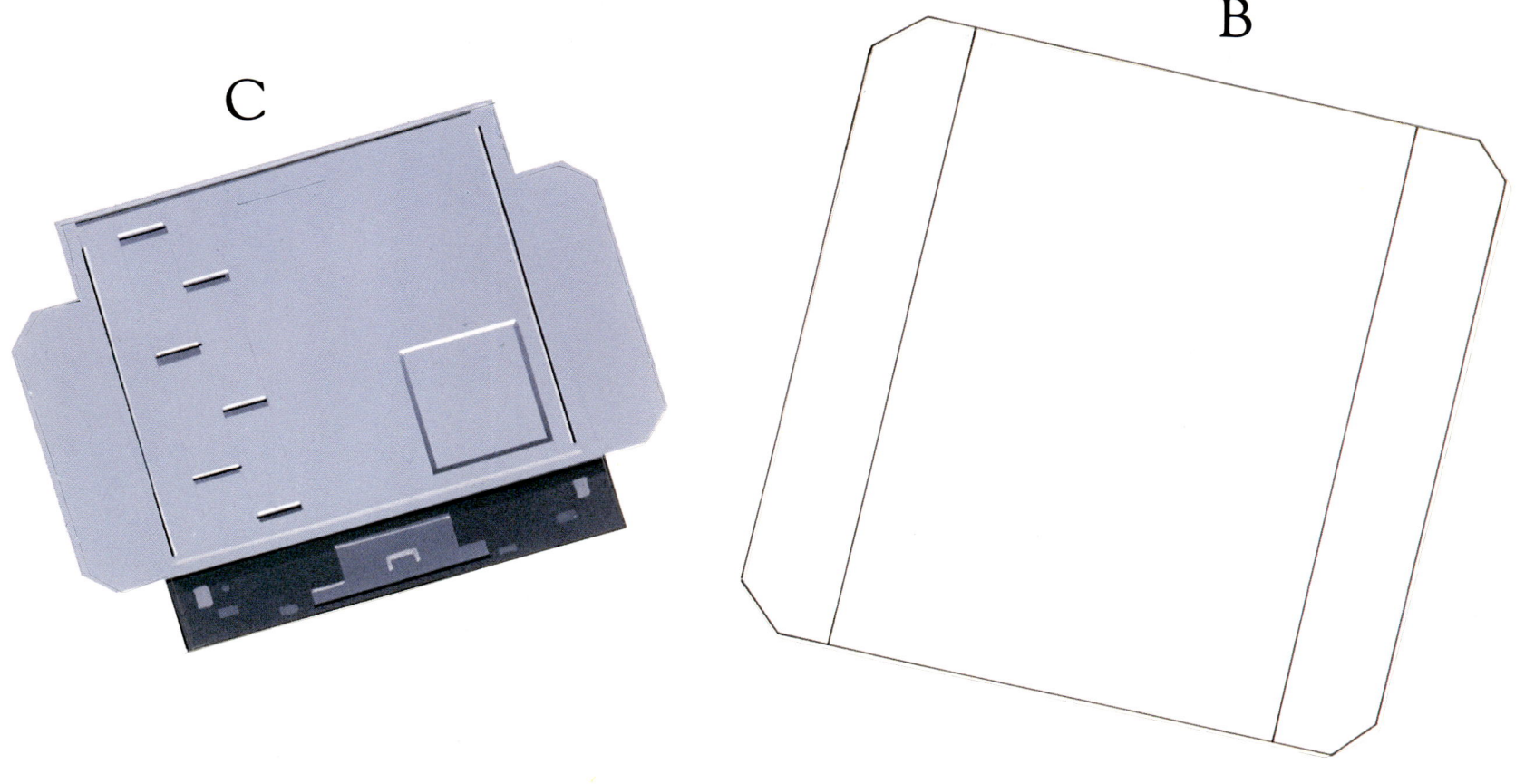

1. Remove all the parts. 2. Fold tender section (A) as shown. 3. Slot strut (B) into section (A). 4. Slot section (C) into end of section (A). 5. Slot tender assembly onto engine.

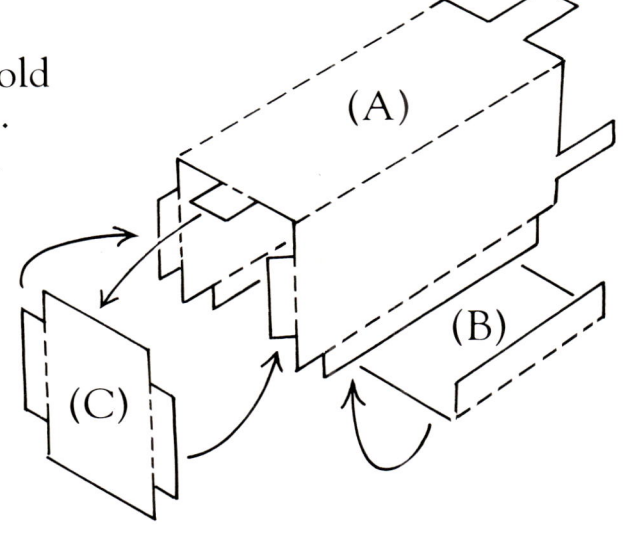

A

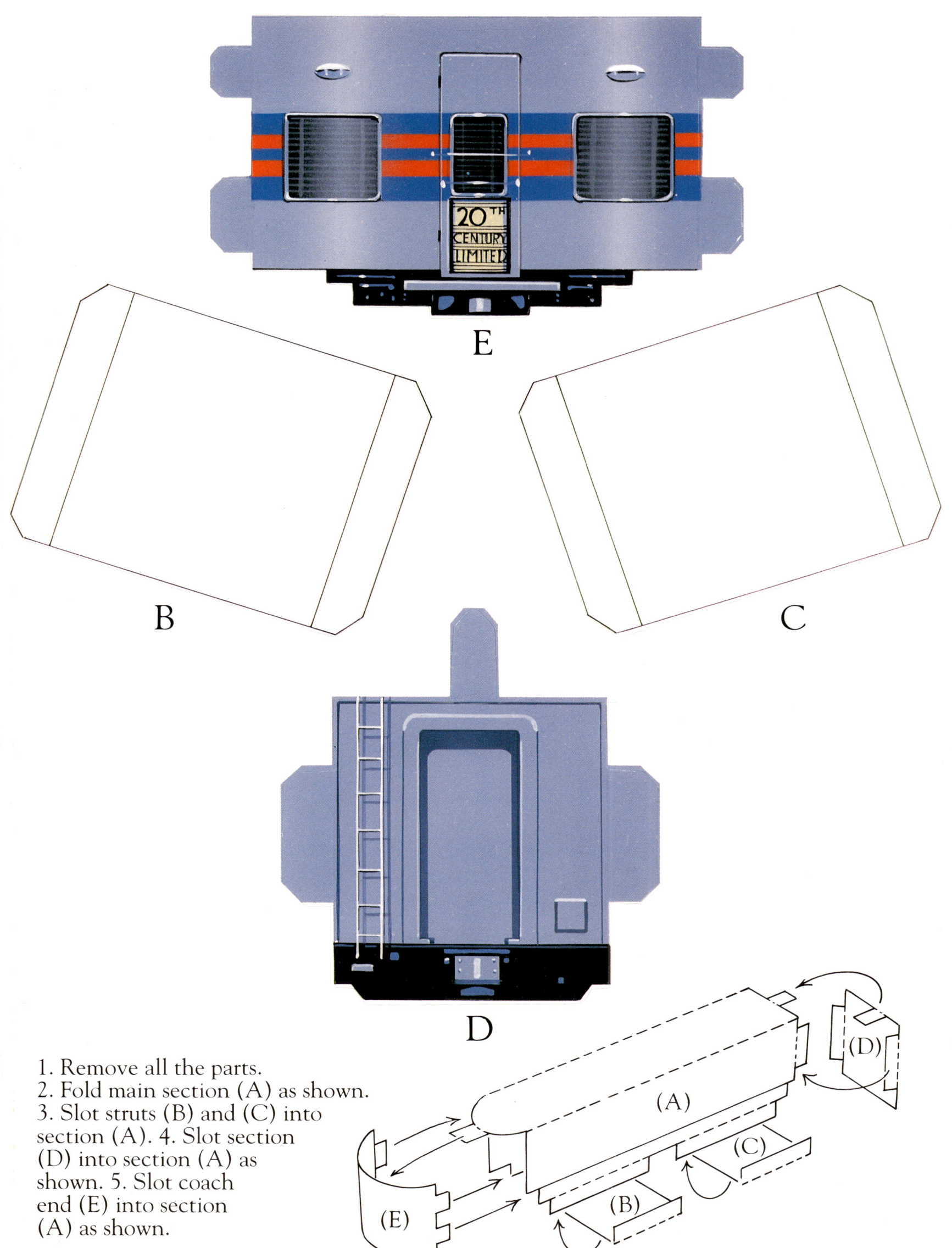

E

B

C

D

1. Remove all the parts.
2. Fold main section (A) as shown.
3. Slot struts (B) and (C) into section (A). 4. Slot section (D) into section (A) as shown. 5. Slot coach end (E) into section (A) as shown.

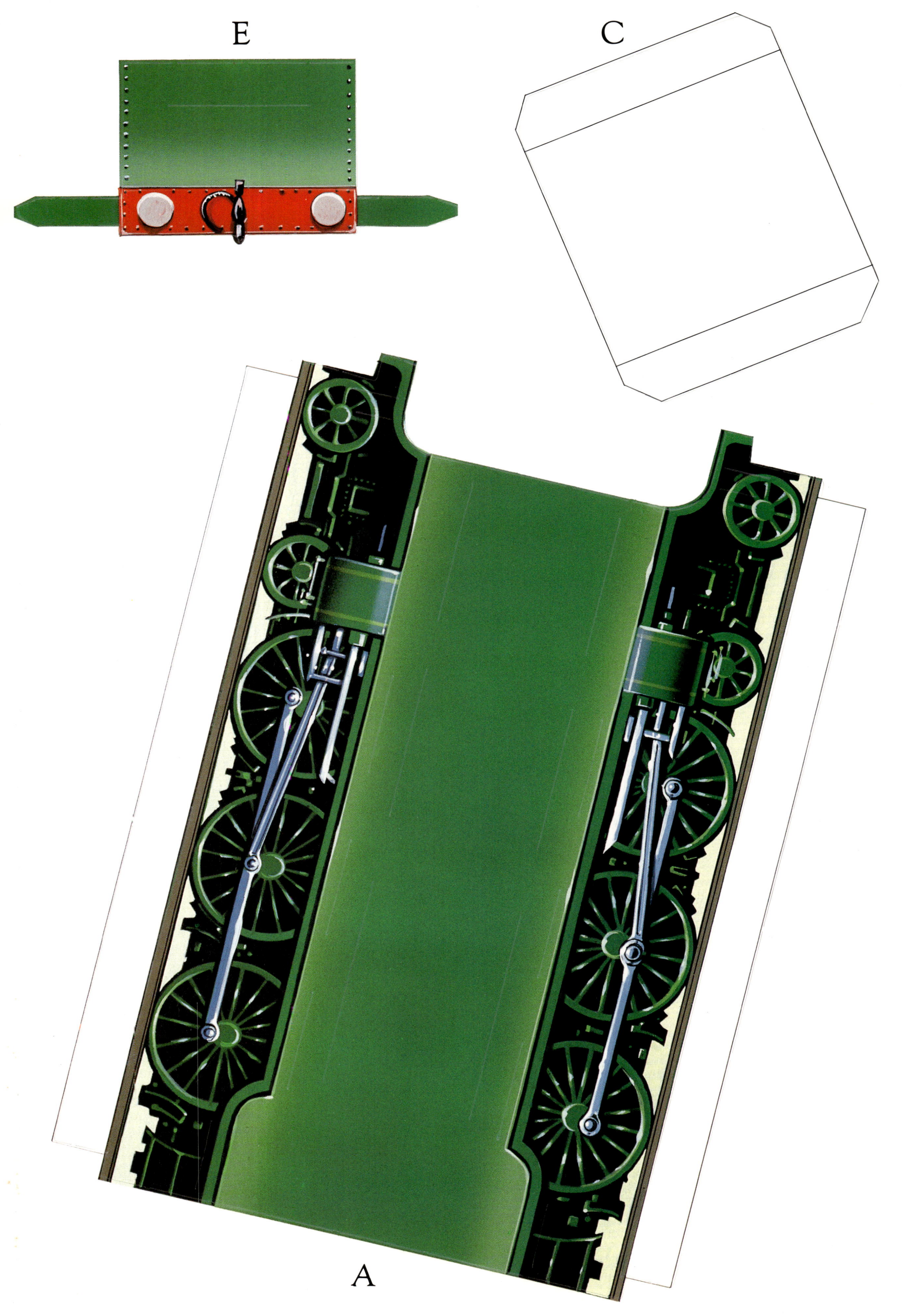

E

C

A

Lift gate-fold

Lift gate-fold

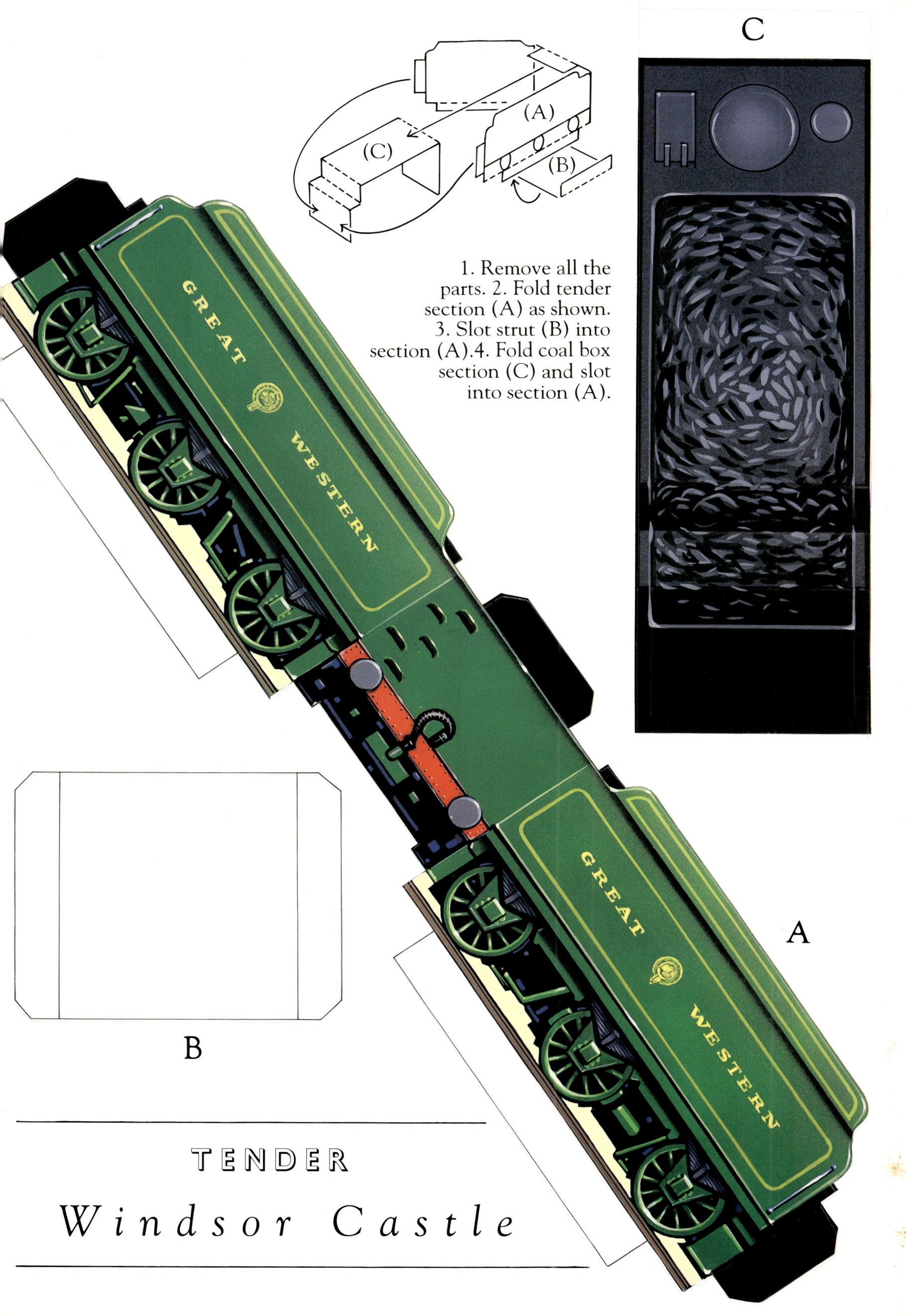

C

1. Remove all the parts. 2. Fold tender section (A) as shown. 3. Slot strut (B) into section (A). 4. Fold coal box section (C) and slot into section (A).

(A)

(C)

(B)

A

B

TENDER

Windsor Castle

A

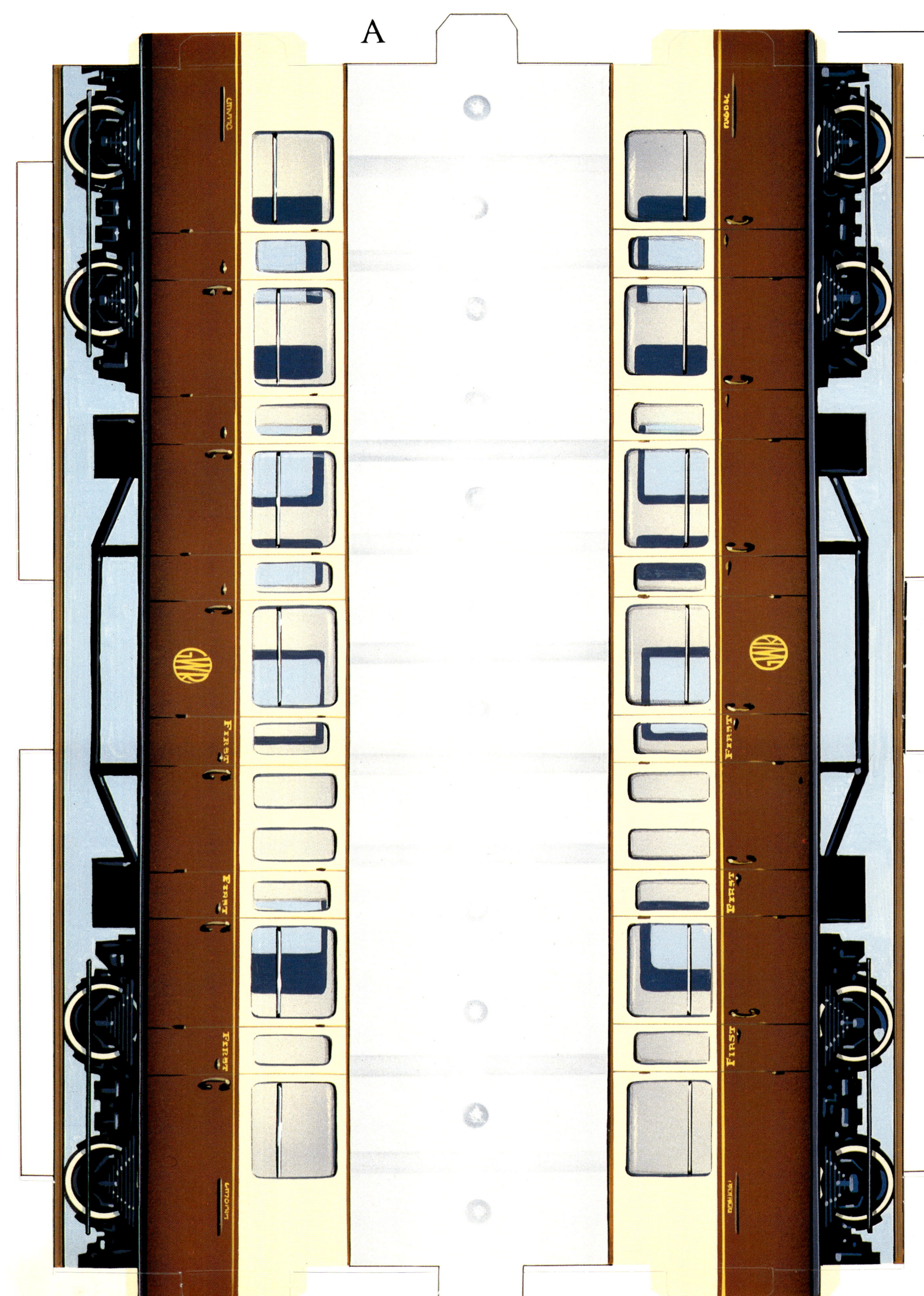

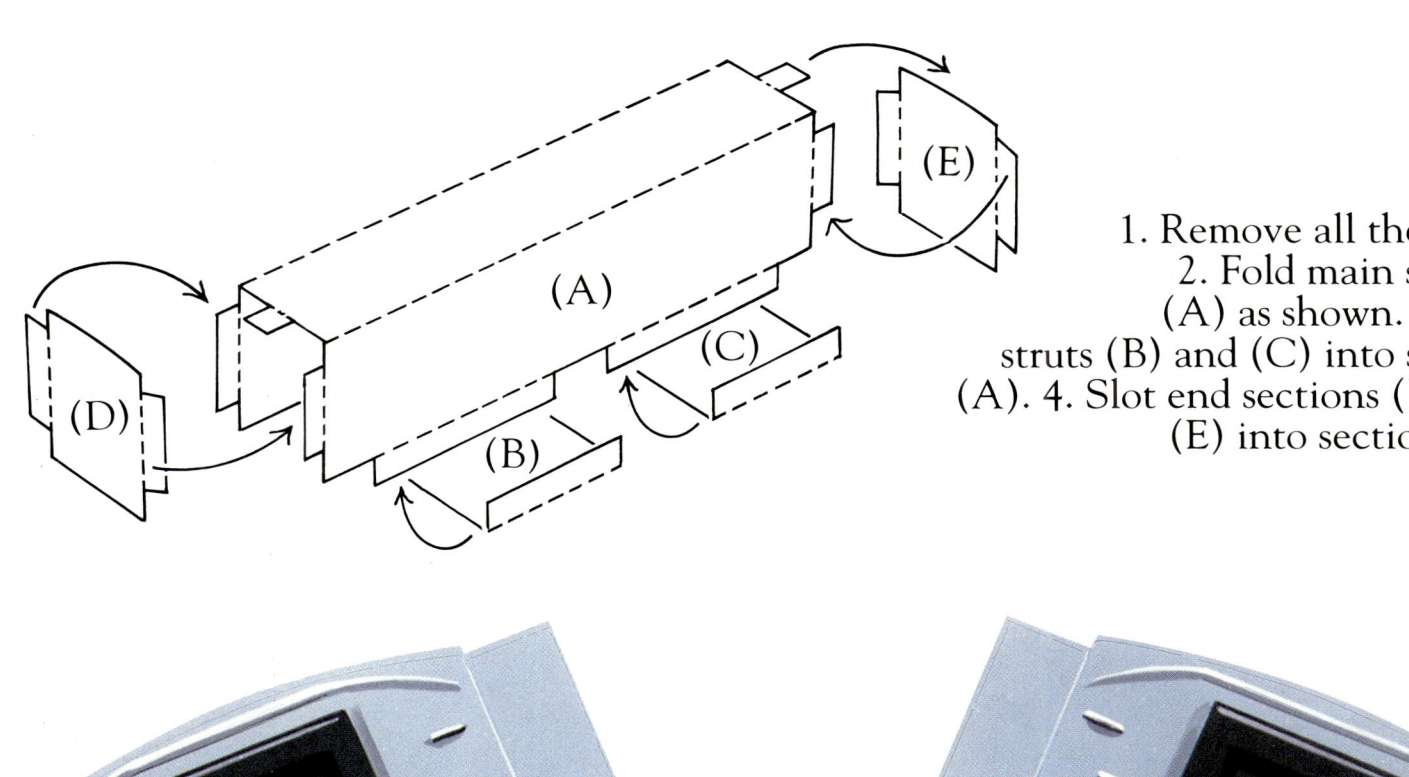

1. Remove all the parts. 2. Fold main section (A) as shown. 3. Slot struts (B) and (C) into section (A). 4. Slot end sections (D) and (E) into section (A).

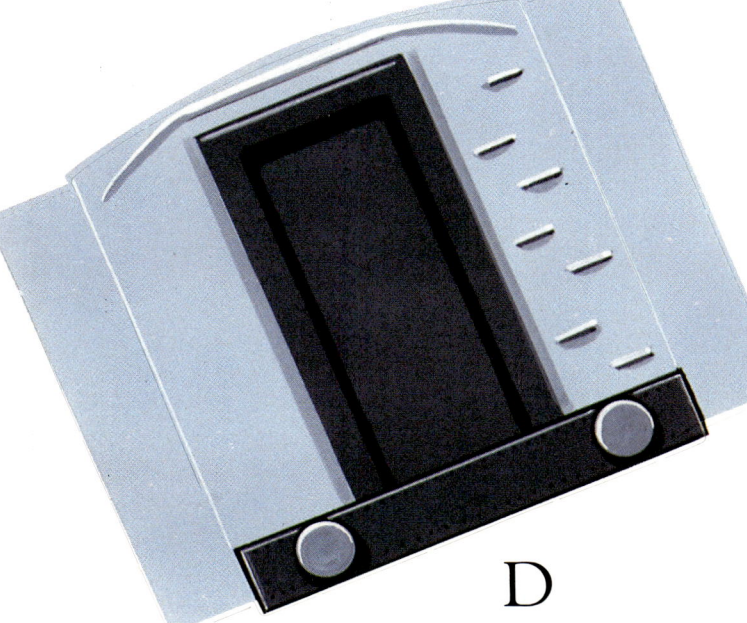

D

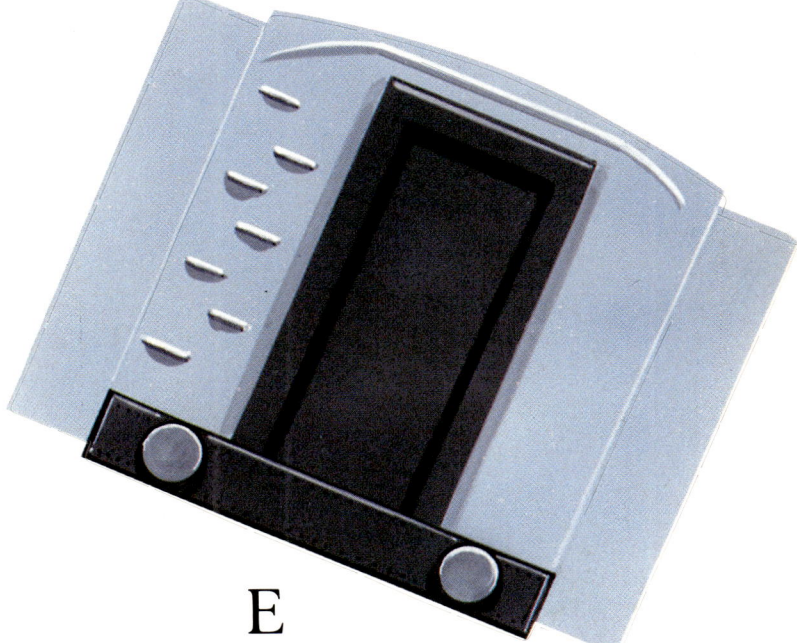

E

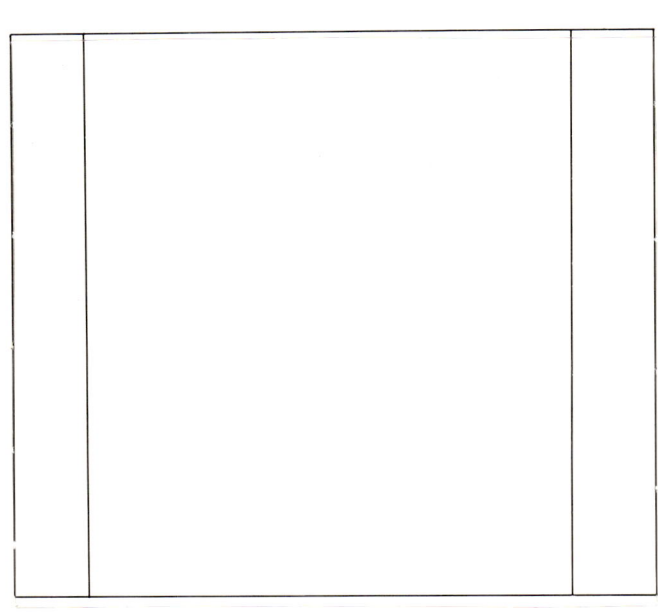

B

C

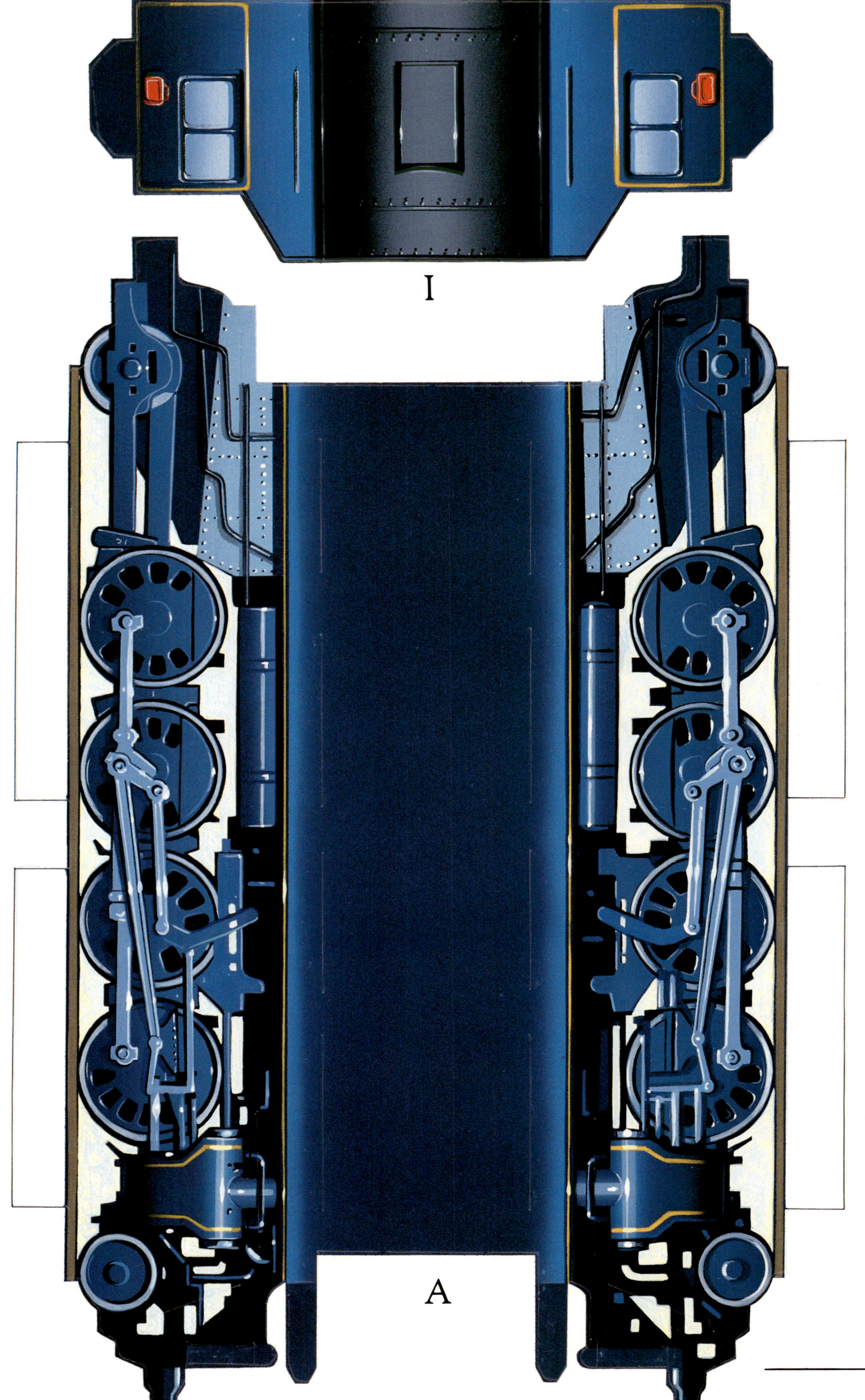

I

A

Lift gate-fold

Lift gate-fold

A

TENDER

Orient Express

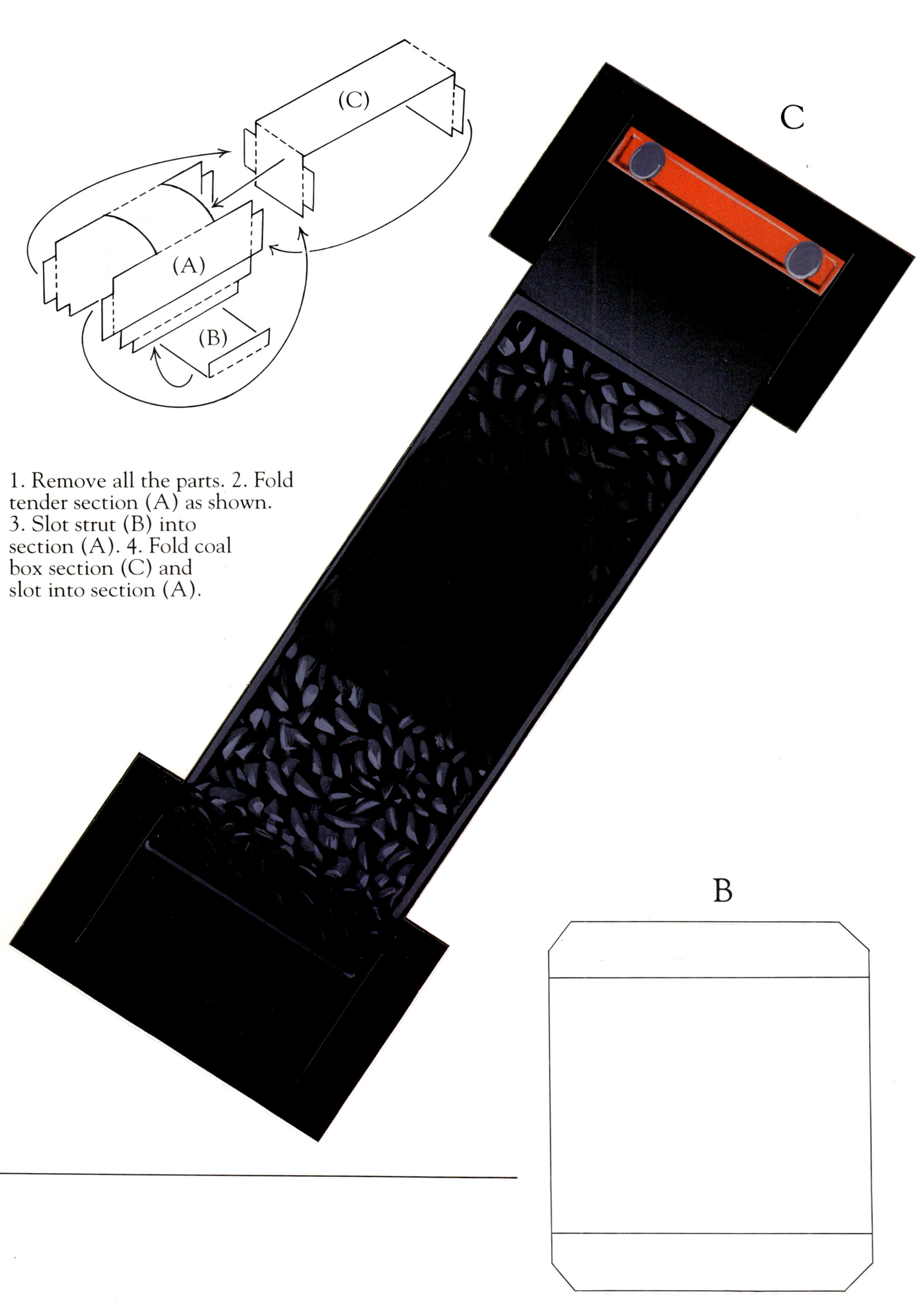

1. Remove all the parts. 2. Fold
tender section (A) as shown.
3. Slot strut (B) into
section (A). 4. Fold coal
box section (C) and
slot into section (A).

A

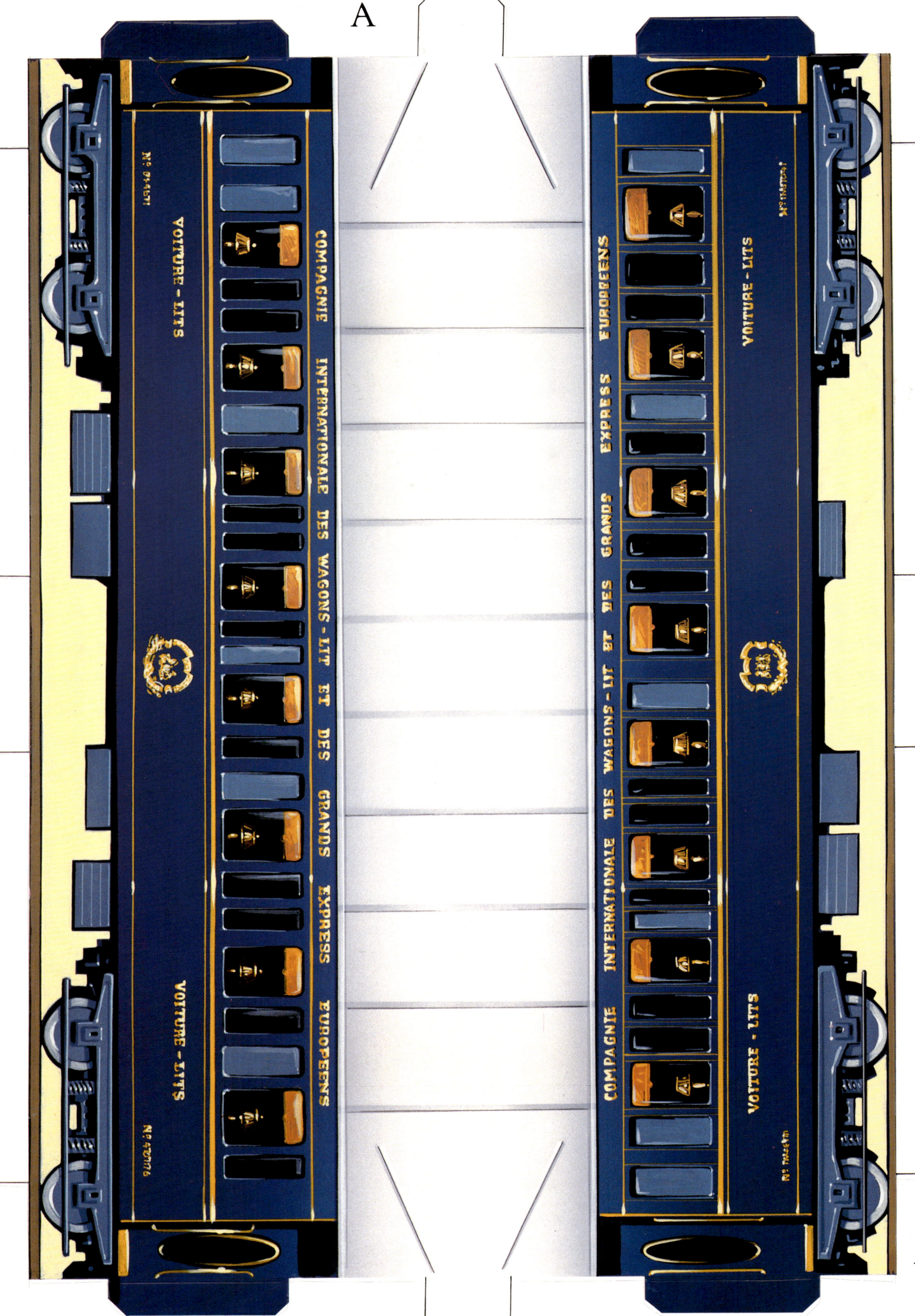

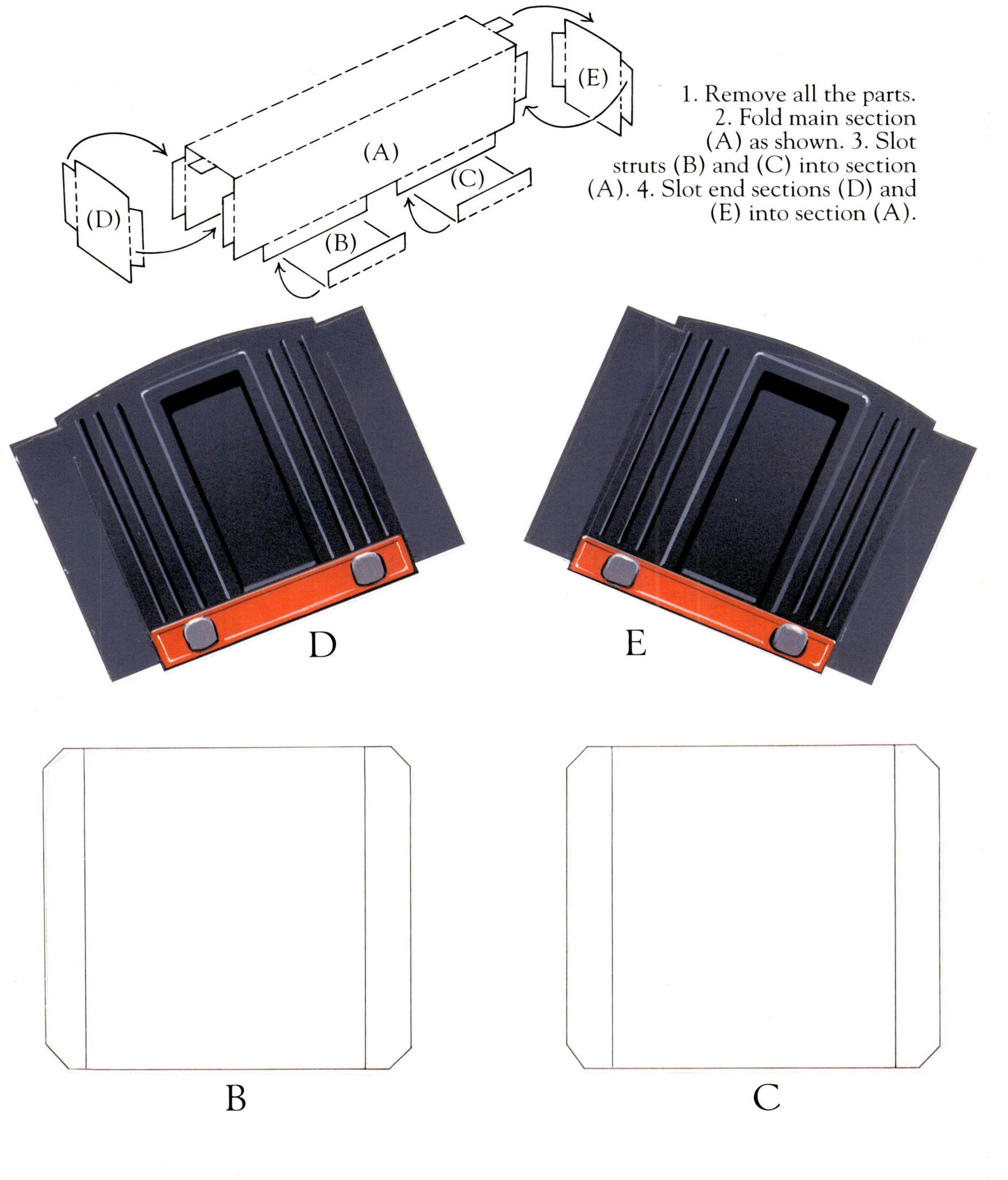

1. Remove all the parts.
2. Fold main section (A) as shown. 3. Slot struts (B) and (C) into section (A). 4. Slot end sections (D) and (E) into section (A).

(A)

(B)

(C)

(D)

(E)

D

E

B

C

Orient Express

A4 PACIFIC CLASS 4-6-2 STREAMLINED LOCOMOTIVE

The Mallard

The Mallard is famous for setting the world speed record for a steam engine – a record it still holds. *The Mallard* achieved an amazing 126 miles per hour on July 3 1938, as part of a Westinghouse Brake Company test train.

Designed for the London and North Eastern Railway (L.N.E.R.) by the legendary locomotive engineer Sir Nigel Gresley, a total of 35 A4 Pacific Class engines were built at Doncaster, Yorkshire. Each engine and tender together were a total of 71 feet 6 inches long, 13 feet 1 inch tall, and weighed 167 long tons.

Six Pacific Class engines are still in full working order, including the *Dwight D. Eisenhower* in the United States. *The Mallard* has been restored with its distinctive L.N.E.R. garter-blue exterior, and is displayed at the British Transport Museum.

The passenger coach depicted in this book is the standard 65-foot British Pullman car of the period. Its interior was luxuriously furnished in walnut and velvet.

J CLASS HUDSON 4-6-4 STREAMLINED LOCOMOTIVE

The 20th Century Limited

When the New York Central railroad introduced its striking, aerodynamic J Class Hudsons in 1938, it gave America some of its finest and fastest trains.

In active service from 1938 to 1956, a total of 50 Hudsons were built. But only 10 of these engines were constructed with distinctive torpedo-shaped fronts, courtesy of designer Henry Dreyfuss. One of these streamlined beauties, *The 20th Century Limited*, turned heads on its 16–1/2 hour run between New York and Chicago. New York Central crews competed for the privilege to drive these trains, which cruised at up to 80 miles per hour.

The Hudsons were massive machines. Each engine weighed 230 tons; each tender carried 46 tons of coal and 18,000 gallons of water. Hudson engines were able to haul luxury trains of up to 18 coaches, including diners, sleeping cars, and the stylish Dreyfuss-designed observation car featured in this book. This round-ended coach was positioned at the rear of the train and featured a modern interior with venetian blinds, restful colors, and club chairs.

CASTLE CLASS 4-6-0 EXPRESS LOCOMOTIVE

The Windsor Castle

The Castle Class engines were powerful workhorses for Britain's Great Western Railway (G.W.R.). Known affectionately as "God's Wonderful Railway," the G.W.R. main lines were constructed by the innovative Victorian engineer Isambard Kingdom Brunel. The first section, linking London to Bristol, was opened in 1835.

The Castle Class locomotives were designed by C.B. Collett. A total of 155 were produced between 1923 and 1951 at G.W.R.'s huge workshops at Swindon, a town 77 miles due west of London. On its completion in 1924, the Castle Class engine depicted here, *The Windsor Castle*, was driven personally from the workshops to Swindon Station by King George V.

Castle Class engines weighed 126 tons. Each engine and tender has a combined length of 65 feet 2 inches and a height of 13 feet 5 inches. The great power of the Castle Class engines allowed them to claim the title of "the fastest trains in the world" during the 1930s. On one occasion, *The Tregenna Castle*, one of *The Windsor Castle's* sister engines, hauled a train 77.5 miles in 56 minutes – an average speed of almost 83 miles per hour.

The passenger coach in this book is typical of G.W.R.'s rolling stock. Painted an attractive brown and cream, they were also designed by Collett.

141 R
2-8-2
MIKADO
LOCOMOTIVE

The Orient Express

The founder of the Wagons Lits Company, Georges Nagelmackers of Belgium, had been enthralled by railways from an early age. In the United States he met George Mortimer Pullman, the American inventor and train designer. Together they decided to build a train like a Grand Hotel on wheels.

Their creation, *The Orient Express*, set a standard of train travel luxury that has never been equalled. From the 1920s through the 1940s, the famous *Orient Express* crossed Europe pulled by a variety of locomotives. The Mikado locomotive featured in this book was one of them. It was an American design with French styling. This magnificent engine weighed 175 tons with its tender; combined they were 78 feet 6 inches long and 13 feet 9 inches high.

During its heyday, the *Orient Express* carried royalty, diplomats, and film stars on the run from Paris to Istanbul. The 70-foot coaches had sophisticated blue and gold exteriors, and featured Lalique crystal and wood marquetry panels inside. The train has been featured in many works of literature (including, of course, Agatha Christie's *Murder on the Orient Express*). Many of the original coaches have been restored and now form part of the reinstated *Orient Express* line service, which currently runs from London to Venice via Dover and Calais. The modern *Orient Express* is powered by electric locomotives.